The Magic Footprints

Melissa Balfour * Russell Julian

EGMONT
We bring stories to life

First published in Great Britain 2005
by Egmont UK Ltd
239 Kensington High Street, London W8 6SA
Text copyright © Melissa Balfour 2005
Illustrations copyright © Russell Julian 2005
The author and illustrator have asserted their moral rights.
Paperback ISBN 978 1 4052 1794 1
7 9 10 8
A CIP catalogue record for this title is available from the British Library.
Printed in U.A.E.

Tim's
Birthday

Lola's
Present

Surprise!

For Gabriel,
love Mummy.

For Phillip and Glenys Julian,
my mum and dad,
R.J.

Tim's Birthday

It was Tim's birthday. Wig and Zip

gave him a perfect blue plane.

They put on party hats. Tim played
with his plane.

He blew out all the candles on his cake.

Somebody was watching Tim and

Wig and Zip. Somebody new.

Tim played with his plane.

It did loop the loops.

Tim dropped his plane.

Somebody laughed.

'Hello,' said Somebody.

Tim's plane flew behind a chair.

'I'm Lola,' said Lola.

Tim's plane flew behind a tree.

Tim's plane peeped out. Then Tim
peeped out. Lola had gone.

The doorbell rang.

It was Lola. 'Happy Birthday!'

I hope you like it.

17

'Goodbye, Lola.'

Lola's Present

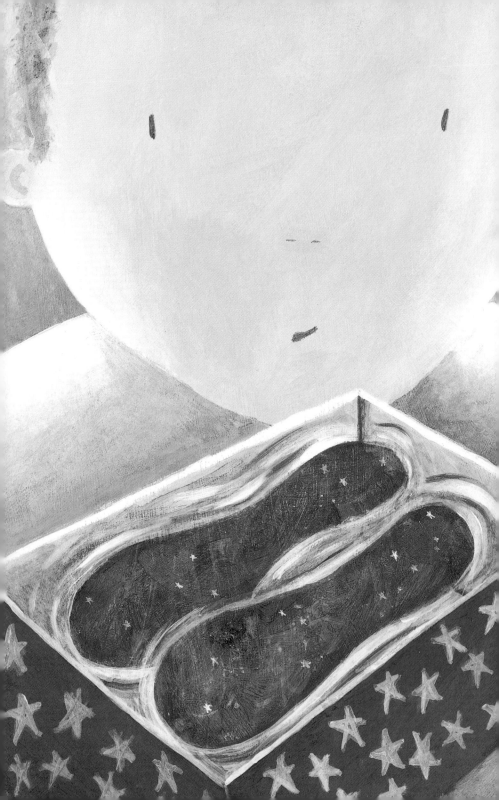

Tim opened his present.

Lola had given him footprints.

Tim left them in the box. He played with his plane.

Tim liked his plane best.

It could fly up in the sky . . .

really high . . .

turn upside down . . .

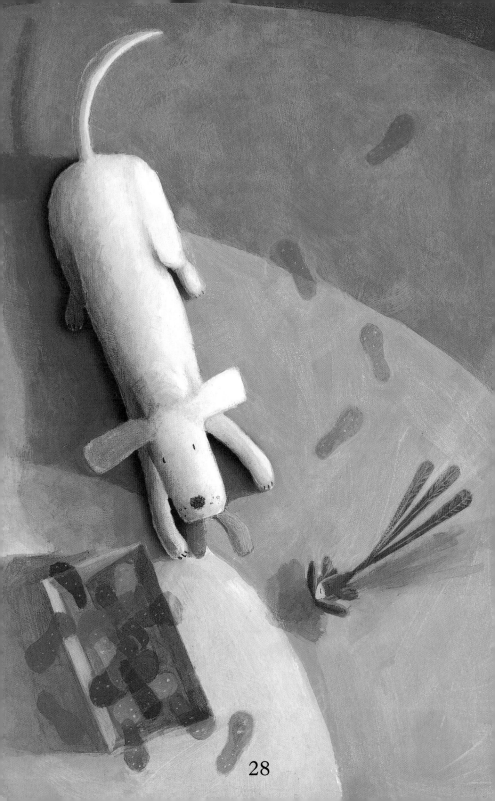

and land on the water.

It was bedtime.

Wig put the footprints in Zip's cage.

Tim noticed his footprints.

He was surprised.

Tim opened the cage door.

Then he got into bed.

Surprise!

In the night, Tim woke up.

His footprints were gone.

He looked out of the window.

They were in the garden!

Tim went into the night.

He followed his footprints . . .

Tim's footprints flew out of his hands.

They flew up in the sky . . .

. . . and into Lola's garden.

There they are.

Lola and Tim followed them.

They climbed over the fence.

The footprints were flying over

the pond.

Lola and Tim looked in the pond.

The footprints were jumping.

Zip caught one in his beak.

43

Tim went fishing for footprints.

So did Lola.

You've got one!

Wig barked. A light had gone on

in Lola's house.

Goodnight, Lola.

Goodnight, Tim.